SCOOBY DOO 2

MONSTERS UNLEASHED

Adapted by
Tracey West

WORLDWIDE PUBLISHING

SCHOLASTIC INC.

New York Toronto London Auckland Sydney
Mexico City New Delhi Hong Kong Buenos Aires

ISBN 0-439-56879-X

Designed by Louise Bova

12 11 10 9 8 7 6 5 4 3   4 5 6 7 8 9/0

Printed in the U.S.A.

First printing, March 2004

"Check it out, Scooby," said Shaggy. "This is our big night!"

Shaggy, Scooby, Daphne, Velma, and Fred waved to the crowd. They were guests at the opening of a new museum.

A news reporter talked to the gang. "I am here with Mystery, Inc.," said the reporter, Heather. "Inside the museum you can learn about all of their old cases."

The gang stepped inside the museum.
It was filled with costumes of the monsters
and ghosts they had captured.

Shaggy shivered. "Do you remember when Chickenstein tried to pluck us?" he asked.

"Don't be afraid," Daphne said. "They are just costumes. They are not real."

CHICKENSTEIN

But then the lights went out.
Crash! The Dinosaur Ghost came to life!
It flew around the room. People screamed
and ran.

Shaggy and Scooby tried to tie up the ghost. But they got tied up instead!
The ghost flew to a strange man in a mask.

"You are fools, Mystery, Inc.!" said the man in the mask.

The Dinosaur Ghost swooped down on Shaggy and Scooby again.

Then the ghost and the man in the mask got away.

Later, the gang watched the whole thing on the news.

"The Dinosaur Ghost stole costumes from the museum," said Heather. "Mystery, Inc. could not stop it!"

Shaggy and Scooby felt terrible. It was all their fault!

"We have to stop messing up, Scoob," said Shaggy. "From now on, we will be the best detectives ever!"

"Right!" Scooby said.

Back in the lab, Velma looked for clues.
"The first Dinosaur Ghost was Dr. Jacobo," she said.

"Maybe he brought the ghost to life," said Fred.

"No," Velma said. "Dr. Jacobo went to jail. He tried to get away. But he was lost at sea."

"What about his friend, Old Man Wickles?" asked Daphne.

"Hmm," said Fred. "That could be. Old Man Wickles used to be the Black Knight Ghost."

"We caught Old Man Wickles in an old mine. It was right here in Coolsville!" said Daphne. "Maybe we should check it out."

Shaggy had an idea. He and Scooby snuck off to the mine on their own.

They saw Old Man Wickles! He went into an old mine shaft.

They followed Old Man Wickles into a strange room. It was filled with crazy machines. Scooby opened up a box filled with bottles.

"Mmmmm," he said. "Rogurt!"

Scooby took a sip. Then he turned into a monster!

"Like, yikes!" Shaggy said. "We have to fix you, Scoob."

Shaggy gave Scooby another bottle to drink. But this time Scooby changed into a super smart geek!

Some of it spilled on Shaggy. He grew big and strong.

Super smart Scooby knew just what to do. He made a potion to change them back to normal.

Finally, Velma, Fred, and Daphne found Shaggy and Scooby.

They looked in another room.

"Every costume from the museum is here," said Fred. "Someone is using the costumes to make real monsters!"

"It is dark in here," said Shaggy.
"Scooby, turn on the lights."
Scooby-Doo pulled a switch.
"Ruh-roh!" Scooby said.
It was the wrong switch. More monsters
came to life!

Two scary monsters chased Shaggy and Scooby.

"Oh man!" Shaggy said. "These monsters really have eyes for us!"

Shaggy and Scooby raced into the Mystery Machine.

"We took this control panel from the monster factory," said Velma. "Now we need to find out how to stop those monsters!"

The gang returned to their old high school clubhouse. Velma, Fred, and Daphne went to the lab. They were trying to fix the control panel.

Shaggy and Scooby were sad.

"This is all our fault," Shaggy said. "We messed up again!"

Velma, Daphne, and Fred changed the control panel.

"We have to get back to the monster factory," said Velma. "We can use the new control panel to stop the monsters."

The gang got back in the Mystery Machine.
But they did not get very far.
   The Dinosaur Ghost attacked again! It
grabbed Fred and Daphne.
   "Scooby, you drive the van!" Fred yelled.

More monsters attacked. Velma gave the control panel to Shaggy.

"It is up to you and Scooby now," she said.

Shaggy shook his head. "Not us! We will mess up."

"You can do it, guys!" Velma said. "I am counting on you!"

Shaggy and Scooby ran for the monster factory. They had to go through the dark mine first. Then they heard a roar. A monster ran after them.

"I am the Cotton Candy Glob!" yelled the monster.

A monster made of candy? "We know just what to do with you!" Shaggy said.

They came out of the mine a few minutes later.

"Now I am thirsty!" said Shaggy.

The masked man from the museum appeared again! He sent more monsters after Shaggy and Scooby.

They leaped over the monsters. Then Shaggy threw the control panel to Scooby.

Scooby caught it! He plugged the panel into the monster-making machine.
Zap! All of the monsters vanished.
"We did it, Scoob!" Shaggy cheered.

"Now let's see who this masked man is," said Velma.
She took off the mask.
"It's Heather, the news reporter!" Daphne said.

"I am not done yet," Velma said. She took off another mask.

"It is Dr. Jacobo," said Velma. "He was not lost at sea after all."

"Rats!" said Dr. Jacobo. "I wanted to make you kids look like losers. But I guess it did not work."

"Thanks to Shaggy and Scooby," Velma said.
"We could not have done it without you."
"Did you hear that, Scoob?" Shaggy said.
"We did it! We *are* good detectives!"
"Rooby-rooby-roo!" Scooby cheered.